Hank
THE
COWDOG.

LOST IN THE
BLINDED BLIZZARD

John R. Erickson

Illustrations by Gerald L. Holmes

Maverick Books
Published by Gulf Publishing Company
Houston, Texas

Maverick Books
Published by Gulf Publishing Company
P.O. Box 2608; Houston, Texas 77252-2608

10   9   8   7   6   5   4   3   2

Library of Congress Cataloging-in-Publication Data
Erickson, John R., 1943–
Hank the cowdog lost in the blinded blizzard / John R. Erickson ;
illustrations by Gerald L. Holmes.
    p.   cm.
Summary: While battling a "blinded" blizzard to get cough syrup
for Baby Molly, fearless Hank charms Miss Beulah the Collie Dog,
saves Slim and Drover from freezing, sings a love song about fleas,
and outwits Pete the Barncat.
    ISBN 0-87719-196-4 (hbk.).—ISBN 0-87719-192-1 (pbk.).—
0-87719-193-X (cassette)
    1. Dogs—Fiction.   [1. Dogs—Fiction.   2. Ranch
life—Fiction.   3. West (U.S.)—Fiction.   4. Humorous stories.]   I.
Holmes, Gerald L., ill.   II. Title.
PS3555.R428H327   1991
813'.54—dc20
[Fic]   90-25861
                                                                    CIP
                                                                     AC

Hank the Cowdog is a registered trademark of John R. Erickson.

Printed in the United States of America

C O N T E N T S

Have you read all of Hank's adventures?
Available in paperback at $6.95:

All books are available on audio cassette too!
($15.95 for two cassettes)

Also available on cassettes:
Hank the Cowdog's Greatest Hits!

Volume 1 Product #MB4120	$6.95
Volume 2 Product #MB4137	$6.95
Volume 3 Product #9194	$6.95

CHAPTER
1

MYSTERIOUS RINGING
IN THE NIGHT

I t's me again, Hank the Cowdog. It was a cold, windy night in February. It had begun to snow and the cowboys were worried that it might turn into a blizzard.

It did, one of the worst blizzards I'd ever seen.

As I lay there in front of the stove in Slim's house, little did I know that within a matter of hours I would have to leave the warmth and security of the house and go out alone into the teeth of the blinded blizzard and perform an errand of mercy.

I didn't know all that, and you're not supposed to know it either. It comes later in the story but I kind of blurted it out without thinking.

I shouldn't have done that. Forget I said it.

Okay. Drover and I had gone down to Slim's place to spend the night, but let me hasten to add that our going down to Slim's place had *nothing whatever* to do with the fact that he allowed us dogs to sleep inside in front of his woodstove.

See, I really don't approve of sleeping indoors, and I've never had much use for . . .

All right, maybe the sleeping-indoors-beside-the-stove factor had played a small part in our decision to camp out with Slim that night, but only a very small part.

Mainly, I thought that he needed some company and also the security that comes from having the Head of Ranch Security close at hand.

No kidding, that was the main reason.

Well, it was along about nine o'clock. Slim had been sitting in his big rocking chair and reading a livestock magazine, while we dogs, uh, guarded the stove.

You never know when some nut will try to steal your stove.

All at once, Slim stood up and yawned. "Boys, all this excitement is about to wear me out." He fished out his pocket watch. "Good honk, it ain't but nine o'clock and I'm already fightin' to stay awake."

He wandered into the kitchen and opened up the icebox and pulled out the makings for a ketchup and bread sandwich. When he took the first bite, ketchup oozed out the back side. It looked pretty awful.

He gnawed it down to a stub, licked his fingers,

and pitched the stub over in our direction — two little corners of bread splattered with ketchup.

I sniffed it and, shall we say, turned it down. Even Drover, who will eat anything that doesn't eat him first, even Drover turned it down.

We whapped our tails on the floor and tried to express our deepest sorrow at turning down Slim's offer of stale bread crusts. At the same time, I tried to let him know that I might consider a better offer — say, sardines, Vienna sausage, a piece of cheese, or any one of the many varieties of fresh meat that might have been tucked away in his freezer compartment.

This was a delicate situation that required near-perfect coordination between tail-whapping and a sad look in the eyes. I thought I'd pulled it off pretty well, but Slim missed it.

"Dumb dogs," he said, and built another ketchup sandwich.

Suddenly and all at once, with no warning whatsoever, the lights went out and we were plunged into total darkness, except for the little flare of light that showed through the air vent on the stove.

I could hear Slim mumbling to himself in the kitchen. "Well, there goes the electric. We must have gotten five snowflakes. That's usually what it takes. Now, where'd I put the candles?"

In the process of stumbling around to find a candle,

he kicked over the sack of garbage that had been sitting beside the stove for two or three weeks.

"Dadgum garbage. You'd think somebody around here would take it out to the barrel."

He found a stub of candle in one of the cabinets and struck a wooden match with his thumbnail. Pretty good trick, as long as you don't get burning sulphur under the nail, but he did, and that seemed to wake him up.

That was the first time I'd ever seen a grown cowboy sucking his thumb.

He lit the candle and then went looking for his coal-oil lamp, which he found and lit with the candle. Holding the lamp about shoulder high, he went to the front door and looked out. "Dogs, that old wind is gettin' up. If it should happen to start snowing hard, we'd be in for a blizzard, sure 'nuff."

He set the lamp down and had just lowered himself into the rocking chair when, all of a sudden and out of nowhere, a bell began to ring. I shot a glance at Drover.

"What was that?"

"Sounded like a bell to me."

"Exactly. But there are no bells in this house."

It rang a second time.

"There it goes again, Hank! What does it mean?"

"It means," I pushed myself up from the hearth and switched all my Hair Lift-Up circuits over to manual, "it means that the time has come for us to BARK. I don't know what that thing is or where it came from, Drover, but a dog can never go wrong by barking."

And so we barked. We threw ourselves into the . . .

Okay, in my original analysis, I had more or less forgotten that Slim had a telephone in his house and that telephones make a ringing sound — but not all the time. That's the crucial point.

See, those telephones will lurk in silence for hours and sometimes even days, and just about the time you've forgotten about 'em, they'll stop lurking and start ringing.

And for that reason, I've never trusted a telephone. There's something just a little sneaky . . . I don't like 'em, is the point.

It took Slim a couple of minutes to find the phone. It had gotten lost beneath the shifting whispering sands, so to speak, of his living room — meaning that it had been buried beneath back issues of *Livestock Weekly*, dirty socks and old shirts, picture-show calendars, and other items too numerous to mention.

It rang and rang, and we barked and barked. On the fifth ring, Slim found the cord and pulled on it until the phone appeared out of the rubble.

He gave me a wink and said, "They can't fool me." He put the phone to his ear. "Hello. Yes. Yes. No, I wasn't in bed. I couldn't find the derned phone. Hold

5

on a second." He scowled at me. "Hank, dry up, will you?"

At that point I figgered that I had barked just about enough, so I quit. I mean, I'd kept the phone from running out of the room, right? And I'd helped Slim find it, right? So I called off the Code Three and...

Was that a mouse sitting on the toe of Slim's boot?

I narrowed my eyes and studied the object on the toe of his . . . yes, it certainly appeared to be a mouse. I shot a glance at Slim.

He didn't see it.

"What? No, I'm babysittin' Loper's dogs tonight and they were barkin' at the telephone. No, I have no idea why a dog would bark at the telephone, but they did." He chuckled. "Yes, I'm very proud. Would you like to buy one of 'em?"

I wasn't paying much attention to the conversation. By that time I had gone into Stealthy Crouch Mode and was moving on silent paws and weaving my way through the clutter — closing the distance between me and the alleged mouse.

Five feet away from the target, I stopped — froze, actually — and asked Data Control for a confirmation of my original sighting. It came back in a matter of seconds: yes indeed, we had us a live mouse at 0205.

Not only was this mouse alive and sitting on the

toe of Slim's boot, but he was *staring at me and wiggling his whiskers.*

Have we discussed mice? I am the sworn enemy of all mice, especially those that stare and wiggle their whiskers.

I mean, you'd think a mouse would have sense enough to run at the approach of a Head of Ranch Security, but this one seemed to think that he owned the place.

Well, he didn't own the place, and I was fixing to send that little feller a message from the School of Hard Knots.

I trimmed out my ears in the Full Alert Position, punched in Manual Lift-up on the hackles circuit, switched all guidances systems over to Smelloradar Control, and began the approach procedure.

Sounds pretty complicated, huh? You bet it is. A lot of your ordinary dogs just go blundering into a combat situation and won't take the time to use their instruments. I mean, they'd probably say that a little mouse wasn't worth all the effort.

Me? I figger that combat is combat, whether you're going up against a Silver Monster Bird or a sneaky little mouse. On my ranch, we take this stuff pretty serious.

Okay, I eased forward two steps — nose out, ears

up, eyes narrowed, hackles raised, tail thrust outward and locked in at the proper angle. (We like to run that tail at about a 20 degree angle on deals like this, although I've gone as high as 25 degrees on a few occasions.)

I stopped and rolled my eyes towards Slim. He wasn't paying any attention to me, which meant that he was unaware of the trespasser on the toe of his boot.

I went to a Manual Eyeball Shift and turned my gaze back to the mouse. He was sitting on his back legs now, staring at me with his beady little eyes and . . . I don't know, biting his fingernails, sucking his thumb, picking his teeth, whatever it is that mice do when they put their paws in their mouth.

That's what he was doing, which was serious enough in itself. But it also appeared that he was *smirking at me*. That little mouse had just made a foolish mistake. No smirk mouses at Hank the Cowdog and tells to live about it.

Slim was talking again. "Yes, the lights went off about five minutes ago, wind must be blowing the lines around. Coal oil? Sure, I've got a gallon of it somewhere, if I can find it. You bet, come on over."

I eased forward another step. The target had not moved. I was now within range. I prepared all systems for launch and punched in the commands to raise lip-shields and arm all tooth-cannons.

G.L. Holmes

All systems were ready. I entered the countdown:
five, four, three, two, one, charge, bonzai!

Mice are quicker than you might suppose, which

probably explains why I missed the stupid mouse and sank my teeth into Slim's boot and set off a very strange chain of events.

CHAPTER
2

HICKORY DICKORY DOCK:
THE MOUSE RAN UP
SLIM'S LEG

I think Slim was startled when I snapped his boot, but that was a small surprise compared to the one that followed when he felt the mouse running up his leg — inside his pants.

His eyes grew as wide as the lenses of his glasses. His eyebrows shot straight up. "Holy smokes, Billy, *I think a mouse just ran up my pant leg!*"

Fellers, in my long and glorious career as Head of Ranch Security, I had witnessed my share of crazy things, but this deal promised to top them all.

Slim dropped the phone and grabbed his left thigh with both hands. Then he jumped two feet into the air and said — and this is a direct quote — he said, "EEEEEE-YOW! Ow, oh, ee, yipes, stop that, help!"

When he lit back on the floor, he was dancing. I

never dreamed he could move so fast. I mean, on an average ranch day, Slim moves around with something short of lightning speed, but he was sure moving now.

He danced. He stamped his feet. He slapped at his legs. He hollered and bellered and made some very odd squeaking sounds. Hopping around the room on his left leg, he tried to pull off his right boot. Then he hopped around on his right leg and tried to pull off his left boot.

No luck there, so he sat down in the middle of the floor and tugged until the left boot came off.

He cut his eyes from side to side. "Where'd he go?" He peeked into the boot. "Maybe . . . EEEEEEEEE-YOW!"

He was on his feet again, but now his hands were tearing at his belt buckle and zipper. He got his left leg out of the jeans and something small and brown hit the floor.

By George, it was the mouse. Slim had finally flushed him out and now it was time for me to go back into action.

"Get 'im, Hank!"

Well, the mouse went bouncing across the room, just as though he had little springs on his legs — funny how a mouse can do that — and I went tearing after him.

Slim fell in behind me, wearing one boot and one sock, dragging his blue jeans that were still attached to his right leg, and swinging a pool cue.

I chased and he swung. Say, he was out to get revenge on that mouse, and if he'd hit the mouse instead of the ceiling light fixture, we'd have had us one splattered mouse.

Instead, we had us one splattered light fixture, and that pretty muchly ended the excitement.

I tracked the mouse all the way down the hall and into the bedroom, where the trail ended at a hole in the baseboard.

Slim had to get the broom and dust pan and sweep up all the busted glass. He sure looked strange, sweeping the floor in his boxer shorts, with his jeans all wadded up around his right ankle.

I returned to the stove and found that Drover had taken over my spot. "Arise and sing, pipsqueak, and move over before I have to amputate one of your legs."

"Murgle skiffer porkchop, what happened?"

"We have given the mice their evening exercise, is what happened, and you're lying in my spot."

His eyes rolled around for a moment, before they finally came into focus. "Who had some nice evening exercise?"

I went nose to nose with the mutt and gave him a growl. *"Move now, talk later."*

"Oh, okay."

He gathered himself up and staggered two steps to the west. I moved into my place of honor, which Drover had warmed up for me, turned around three times in a tight circle, and collapsed. Oh, that felt good!

Warmed by the warmth of a roaring cedar-post fire, I surrendered my grip on the world and prepared myself for a nice, long murgle skiffer in front of the porkchop.

Perhaps I fell into a dream. I heard a lady-dog's voice saying, "Hello Hank, I think I'm madly in love with you."

Mercy me, Miss Beulah the Collie? Yes, there she was before me, in all her glory — the World's Most Beautiful Collie Gal.

"Ah Beulah, at last you've come to your senses! I knew that sooner or later, the pain in your porkchop would murgle you to skiffering."

"I'm Drover."

"Oh no you're not, because if you were really Drover, then I would be . . . " I opened one eye and saw a terrible sight: Drover. "So it's true? You really are Drover?"

"Well, I think so."

"In that case, you've wrecked my dream and brought it crashing down to the floor of reality."

"Yeah, Slim just finished sweeping it up."

I opened both eyes and glared at him. "What are you talking about?"

"Your dream. It made quite a mess."

"Slim was sweeping up my dream? You're not making any sense, Drover, but that didn't stop you from waking me up, did it?"

"I thought you were having some nice evening exercise. That's what you said."

"I did not say that, but never mind, Drover, because unless I'm badly mistaken, a vehicle has just pulled up in front of the house!"

"Boy, I get confused."

"Bark, Drover, and rush to the door! Someone or something has just territrated our penatory!"

And with that, we rushed to the front door and sent up an amazing barrage of barking. That was just in case they had any big ideas about busting down the door and trying to capture the house.

'Course, it very seldom goes that far in real life. Most intruders can be stopped in their tracks by a good strong dose of barking.

I mean, they'll come ripping up to the house like they own the place, and they might even leap out of the car and go charging up to the front porch in a manner that makes you think they're going to tear the door off its hinges.

Your mailmen and your UPS drivers are the very worst about doing this, I mean, they seem to think they've got a right to enter the ranch without permission and start banging on doors.

But once they reach the porch and hear that barking, they begin to realize that there's a dog on duty, and you'll see an amazing change in their behavior.

At that point they might *tap* on the door, or they might call out, "Is anyone home?" But you won't see 'em *banging* on any doors, no siree, because . . .

HUH?

Someone was banging on Slim's front door, and I mean banging loud.

"Open up, in the name of the law! We know you robbed the stage coach, Slim Chance, and we know you're in there. Now come out with your hands up or we'll burn this place to the ground!"

The, uh, deep roar of a bark that had been gathering momentum in my throat changed pitch all of a sudden, as my, uh, throat seemed to contract, so to speak, in response to the, uh, sound of an angry mob on the front porch.

I hadn't exactly prepared myself for an angry mob, don't you see, and while angry mobs of mobsters have never struck fear in my heart, they have never struck courage in my heart either.

After retreating a few steps . . . several steps . . . halfway across the room, I turned to my assistant. "Drover, I'm almost sure they're bluffing, but just in case . . . "

He had vanished.

I caught a glimpse of him, trying to crawl under Slim's chair, but just then the angry mob broke down the door and hundreds of wild-eyed mobsters carrying torches and bloody swords streamed into the house, screaming horrible things and waving their bloody torches and burning swords.

Well, hey, if I'd known they wanted in that bad, I would have . . . I could see that this was going to be a fight to the finish, and it seemed reasonable and honorable that I should postpone the finish as long as . . .

Fellers, I ran!

C H A P T E R
3

THE SWIRLING
KILLER TORNADO

G etting traction on a linoleum floor is a very difficult thing to do, especially when your paws are turning several thousand RPMs per second.

After running in place for a moment, I finally got traction on the stupid linoleum floor in the hallway and moved my line of defense, so to speak, a bit deeper into the house.

Into the living room.

Under the coffee table.

Not far from Slim.

Hmmm. That was odd. The angry mob had busted into the house to get Slim, right? So why wasn't he running for his gun or doing anything to defend himself? And how come he was laughing . . . and pointing at, well, ME?

It didn't make any sense. I mean, if those mobsters really . . .

Have we discussed childish cowboy pranks? There seems to be something about cowboys that draws them to silly, childish acts of behavior. Perhaps there are some people in this world who would consider these outrageous acts funny, but you will find very few dogs who do.

I mean, we try to run our ranches in a businesslike manner. We try to be serious about things and we don't appreciate . . .

Okay, Billy, our neighbor down the creek, turned out to be one of those jokers, a guy who never passed up a chance to goof off and pull a childish prank.

He'd pulled up in front of Slim's place and banged on the door and yelled all that . . . hey, he hadn't fooled me for a minute with that stuff about how Slim had robbed a so-called . . . I mean, we don't have stage coaches around here, right?

But on the other hand, a guy never knows for sure . . . sec, he was *banging on the door*, and I mean really BANGING and YELLING, sounded like a whole mob of . . .

Well, this guy not only took fiendish delight in making noise and scaring people, but he seemed even prouder of himself for scaring the liver out of me and Drover — primarily Drover.

Don't forget who was the first to run and hide. It wasn't me.

Okay, maybe I ran too, but not as fast as Drover.

Billy was very proud of himself for making all that childish noise and violating the privacy of Slim's home, and there for a second or two, I thought he might get a hernia from laughing so hard at . . . well, at me and Drover, but mainly Drover, who had tried his best to crawl under Slim's easy chair.

Remember that I had crawled under the *coffee table*, not under an easy chair, and it's common knowledge that in serious and disastrous situations, such as earthquakes and tornadoes, citizens should take refuge *under the nearest coffee table*.

So there you are. I had done nothing to be ashamed of. Drover, on the other hand, had walked right into their foolish trick and had become the butt of their laughingstock.

Okay. Billy went down to his knees, he was laughing so hard, and Slim was getting more than a few chuckles out of it too.

You might recall that this was the same Slim who, only moments before, had been running around his house, half-naked, and chasing a poor little mouse with a pool cue.

Right. And the same guy who had destroyed the light fixture on the ceiling.

You'll notice that Slim hadn't been nearly as amused by HIS foolish display as he now was by mine . . . ours . . . Drover's, actually, which just goes to prove that small minds take delight in the misfortunes of others.

It really hurt me to see him laughing at Drover that way.

"Call off your dogs, Slim, before they hurt somebody!"

That was Billy. Very funny. Ho, ho, ho.

"Whatever you do, Billy," said Slim between spasms of infantile laughter, "whatever you do, don't try to crawl under that coffee table with Hank! He's a trained killer, and I ain't sure I can hold him back."

Oh, they got a big chuckle out of that! I glared daggers at them. Also snarled at Billy, just to let him know that sticks and stones might break my bones, but his words might get him bitten on the leg, if he ever turned his back on me.

By this time, Drover had poked his head out from under Slim's chair. "Hi, Hank, what you doing under the coffee table?"

"Don't speak to me, you little weasel."

"What's wrong?"

"You know very well what's wrong. Under combat conditions, you ran and left me to defend the house by myself."

"Well, I thought I saw a mouse and I chased him under the chair."

I gave him a withering glare. "Drover, that is a lie, and you know it."

He hung his head. "I know, but it sounds a lot better than the truth. I don't think I can face the truth."

"Go ahead and face it. You'll feel much better."

"No I won't. I'll feel ten times worse."

"Telling the truth is good for the soul."

"Yeah, but telling a lie is good for everything else."

"Try it, Drover, you might be surprised."

"Well . . . all right." He squinted one eye and appeared to be in deep concentration. "Let's see. I ran away and hid under the chair because . . . "

"Yes, yes?"

"I can't say it, Hank, it just hurts too much."

"Take the plunge and say it."

"Oh rats. I ran away and hid under the chair because... I was scared. There! Now everybody knows."

"But that wasn't so bad, was it?"

"I guess not."

"And don't you feel better now?"

He thought about it for a moment, then gave me his patented silly grin. "You know, I do feel better."

"See what I mean? I'll bet you feel ten times better."

"Oh yeah, ten or maybe even eleven. All at once I feel like a terrible burden has been lifted from my shoulders. I feel wonderful!"

I crawled out from under the table, pushed myself up on all fours, and glared down at the runt.

"Well, you have absolutely no right to feel wonderful. Not only did you behave in a cowardly and chicken-hearted manner in a combat situation, but you had the gall, the nerve, the stupidity to admit it!"

"Yeah but . . . "

"Now, you put that burden right back on your shoulders and carry it around for the next 24 hours. That's your punishment for being a chicken-hearted little mutt. And shame on you!"

"I knew I shouldn't have told the truth! Now I feel ten times worse!"

"Yes, but you deserve it, and that should make you feel better about feeling worse. Now, get out from under that chair and stop showing your true colors."

He crawled out and wiped a tear from the end of his nose. "Hank, what were you doing under that coffee table?"

"I, uh, what coffee table?"

"The one you were under."

"Oh, that one. Yes, it's a coffee table."

"I know, but what were you doing under it?"

"What makes you think I was . . . oh yes, I remember now. Drover, because you were cowering under the chair, you missed hearing why Billy came bursting into the house."

"Yeah, I sure did."

"Good. I mean, yes, of course. He came bursting into the house to announce that a tornado had been sighted nearby—a deadly swirling killer tornado."

"No fooling?"

"That's correct. And as you might know, in the event of a tornado, one should take refuge under the nearest coffee table."

His face brightened. "Gosh, then maybe I did the right thing after all, hiding under Slim's chair."

"I'm afraid not, Drover." I placed a paw on his shoulder and looked into his eyes. "There's a huge difference between a coffee table and a chair."

"There is?"

"Yes. You never sit on a coffee table and you never put coffee on a chair."

"Rats. Then I have to go on carrying my burden around?"

"I'm afraid so, Drover, but because of the tornado, we'll shorten your time to twelve hours."

"Gosh, thanks, Hank!"

One of the nice things about this job is that, every now and then, you get the opportunity to involve yourself in the lives of others, to help them understand themselves and life's many twists and turns.

And that makes it all worthwhile.

C H A P T E R
4

A FEW POINTERS
ON MARKING TIRES

I t took Billy and Slim a while to get all the childish laughter out of their systems.

Slim boiled up a pot of coffee and they sat down beside the stove, drinking coffee and recounting every detail of Billy's entrance into the house.

I noticed that my name came up fairly often in this conversation. They would say something about "old Hank," then glance at me and laugh some more.

Seemed to me that they were trying to milk a dead horse. I mean, I hadn't cared much for the experience the first time around, and it didn't get any better the second or third time.

I continued glaring daggers at them, and more than once, when Billy was pointing his big hairy finger at me (he had black hairs growing between the joints of his fingers), I growled at him. (Oh, and he had black hairs growing on the back of his hand, too.)

I never trust a guy with hairy hands.

The best part of this conversation between Slim and Billy came when Billy took a big swig of coffee and found a drownded cricket in the bottom of his cup.

He stared at it for a second, then said, "Slim, I think the protein's running a little high on this coffee of yours."

Slim leaned out in his chair and frowned. "By gollies, it sure is, but it was the same price as the regular."

Billy went to the sink and poured out the last of his coffee. If he had tossed a glance in my direction, he would have noticed a big cowdog smile on my face. The cause of justice had been served.

Well, after the Cricket Incident I began to feel restless and bored. I felt a cold draft blowing across the floor and suspected that Billy had left the door open a crack. I gave Drover the signal to move out, and we went into the hallway to investigate.

Sure enough, the door was open just a crack. I managed to hook a front paw around the door and pulled it open a little wider, and we stepped outside into the storm. I took several deep breaths and gave myself a good shake.

"Drover, a ranch dog has no business spending time inside a house. That stuffy air can ruin a dog quicker than anything."

He was shivering. "Yeah, but that's the kind of ruin I've always wanted to be."

"I'll try to forget you said that, son. Has it occurred to you that Billy's pickup is sitting right in front of us and we haven't marked his tires?"

"Not really. I was thinking about how cold I am."

I shook my head. "Stop feeling sorry for yourself and mark the back tires. I'll take the front."

"But I'm so cold! And this old leg of mine . . . "

"Never mind the leg, Drover. Do your job. I'll meet you back on the porch in two minutes."

I nudged him off the porch with my nose and went right to work. I sniffed out the left front tire and ran a field analysis of the various scents and chemical compounds it contained. My analysis turned up a powerful showing of . . . rubber?

No big surprise there. After all, most tires are made of . . .

I hurried around to the right side and gave it the same careful laboratory analysis. This one proved more interesting. It tested positive for snow, caliche dust, ragweed, sagebrush, and another scent I couldn't quite identify.

It might very well have come from another dog, so I wasted no time in erasing his phoney mark and adding one of my own.

In case you haven't already guessed, I take great pride in my ability to lay a good strong mark on a set of tires. When a vehicle leaves my ranch, I want the world to know where it's been.

Well, it didn't take me long to mark those two front tires. I mean, I'm the same dog who's accustomed to knocking out an entire pickup and stock trailer all by myself, and then rushing to the yard gate to bark at the driver.

That's an eight-tire job. A lot of dogs wouldn't even attempt a job that big, but it's nothing special to me. On your bigger assignments, like the eight-tire deals, a dog's overall physical condition and endurance become a major factory.

Factor, I should say. A major factor.

So I knocked out my tires in record time and went to the porch to wait for Drover. He didn't come. And he didn't come. I looked toward the rear of the pickup and didn't see him.

What was the little mutt doing back there? What was taking him so long?

I hate to wait, so after waiting and hating every second of it and getting bored, I pushed myself up and swaggered to the rear of the pickup. I figgered I'd end up having to mark his tires for him.

I passed the right rear tire and noticed his mark. Well, at least he'd done something. I continued around the back end of the pickup, and there I found him — sitting down and gazing up at the swirling snow, or something in that general direction.

"Drover, if I'd known it was going to take you five minutes to perform a simple procedure, I would have done it myself. What's the deal?"

"Well, I got distracted, Hank."

"I see. In that case, let's talk about distractions. Distractions are one of your problems. You shouldn't allow yourself to be distracted by distractions."

"What about girls?"

"They shouldn't be distracted either. Distractions are a problem for everyone, regardless of age, gender, breed, or national origin."

"Yeah, but what if I got distracted by a girl instead of a distraction?"

"That's no excuse. In our line of work . . . why do you ask?"

"Oh, I just wondered."

"I see. No, when we're on a job, Drover, we've got no time for . . . you're not listening to me."

His gaze seemed to be directed up towards the pickup bed.

"What?"

"I said, you're not listening to me."

"I can't hear you, Hank, I'm being distracted."

"Drover, this is the very problem I'm trying to help you with, but I can't help you if you continue to be distracted."

"I know, but I can't help it."

"In that case, I have no choice but to . . . " I swung

my gaze around and in an upward direction and locked in on . . .

HUH?

Holy smokes, my heart raced, my head swimmed, swammed, swummed, swum, whatever the fool word is. My legs grew weak, my entire body began to tremble and shake and quiver and quake.

My pulse shot up, my breaths came in short bursts, I felt hot and cold at the same time, and little pins and needles of excitement moved down my backbone and out to the end of my tail.

I was losing control of my own destiny. My eyes crossed and I began speaking in tongues.

Fellers, all of a sudden I forgot about giving Drover a lecture on distractions, because all of a sudden I had stumbled onto one of the biggest distractions in the entire world.

I found myself looking up into the big brown eyes and the adoring gaze of MISS BEULAH THE COLLIE!

She was standing at the rear of the pickup bed, looking down at me. Even though it was pretty dark, and snowing hard, I could see the light of love shining in her eyes.

"Hello, Hank. Hello, Drover."

At the mention of his name, Drover lost control of himself. He began rolling around on the ground and kicking his legs in the air.

"Oh my gosh, it's Beulah, I heard her voice with

my own ears, and there she is in the back of the pickup!"

These strange spasms that Drover has from time to time never fail to embarrass me. I mean, a guy should make every attempt to keep his feelings under control, especially if his feelings reveal emotions that are basically chilly and stylish.

Silly and childish, I should say.

On the one hand, I could understand the powerful effect that Miss Beulah's voice had on Drover. Even I felt a certain tingle of excitement. But on the other hand, a guy must resist the temptation to reveal all his cards, so to speak.

In the game of love, if you reveal all your cards, you will soon reach a point where all your cards have been revealed.

I stepped over the little mutt and let my eyes drift up to Miss Beulah's face. "Oh my goodness, I believe we have company. And my goodness again, it turns out to be Miss Beulah!"

Heh, heh. This was the opening shot of what would surely prove to be the final battle for the fortress of Miss Beulah's heart.

And best of all, her stick-tailed bird-dog friend was nowhere in sight.

CHAPTER
5

DRILLED BY A FLEA
IN FRONT OF MISS BEULAH

"Hello, Hank," she said in that honey-smooth voice of hers.

"Hello, Beulah. I must say that I'm surprised to see you out at this time of night, and I'll even admit that it's a pleasant surprise. But I hope you understand that seeing you here tonight is just one of many surprises that I've experienced today."

"Oh really?"

"Yes. This has been a day full of surprises, Beulah, but that's fairly routine. In my line of work, I see many ladies during the course of an average day."

"Is that so?"

"Oh yes. I couldn't possibly keep a count. Many of them come for advice. Many come for sympathy. And many more come for . . . " I arched my left eyebrow. "Well, it seems that I have a small reputation amongst the ladies. In spite of my best efforts to keep my exploits and adventures a secret, the word just seems to get around."

"How interesting!"

"Yes, indeed." Drover was still rolling around and I stepped on his nose. "Oops, sorry about that, son."

"Oh, my heart's about to bust!" he squeaked.

"That was your nose, Drover, and I would appreciate it if you would stop making a spectacle of yourself."

"I can't help it! I saw her face and it struck me deaf and dumb!"

"Her face might have stuck you deaf, Drover, but you were dumb long before she got here." I stepped over him and let my eyes drift up to Beulah again. "You'll have to excuse Drover, ma'am. Unlike me, he lives a sheltered life and rarely comes into contact with, shall we say, *members of the female species.*"

"What a clever way of saying it!" said Beulah.

"Thank you, thank you, but I really can't take much credit for being clever. You won't believe this, Beulah, but those clever remarks just pop into my head and roll off of my lips. I mean, they come without any effort at all — just like raindrops falling from the prairie or wildflowers springing up on the sky."

A small chirp of laughter came from her lovely mouth. "Oh Hank, sometimes I can't tell whether you're teasing or trying to be serious."

*Heh heh. Good. Great. Perfect. You don't ever want
'em to know all your tricks.*

I tossed my head to one side and chuckled. "Ha,
ha, ha. Yes, all the ladies seem to wonder about that,
Beulah: 'Is Hank being serious or is he just a naughty
teaser.' Ha, ha, ha. Oh my, isn't this life a wonderful
mystery! But if I were to reveal the answer, the mystery would vanish, POOF! And . . . "

At that very moment, just as I had the lovely Miss
Beulah eating my hand — eating OUT of my hand, I
should say — I was drilled by a flea.

This was a cruel twist of fate. It couldn't have come
at a worse time. At first I tried to ignore it. I mean,
ignoring pain was nothing new to me, but hey, this
was pain of a new dimension and a higher order of
majesty.

Anyways, I tried to carry on. "If I were to reveal
all my secrets, Miss Beulah, the flea would vanish in
a poof of yikes!"

The flea would not be ignored.

Let me pause here to say a word about fleas. Yes,
they are very small. If a flea is small and if a flea
makes his living by drilling holes in innocent dogs,
then it follows from simple logic that a small flea
uses a small drill to inflict a small hole upon his victim
— which, following the same line of simple logic,
should cause only a small hurt.

Under ordinary circumstances, simple logic is not only simple but also logical, and therefore true. In this case, simple logic is WRONG. Small fleas cause *big hurts*. Don't ask me how or why, but they do, take my word for it.

So there I was, poised beneath Beulah's balcony, so to speak, and charming her with my words and charms, when all at once — WHAMO! This sniveling flea drilled me in the right dorsal hiney, and fellers, he got my attention.

My head shot up, my tail shot up, and suddenly I found myself rolling around on the ground, withering in pain. Writhing in pain, I should say.

Oh hurt! Oh pain! Oh humiliation!

And of the three, the humiliation was the hardest to bear. Just think about it. You're Head of Ranch Security. You run the place, you're in charge, you're the guy who barks up the sun in the morning and barks it down at night. Nothing, and I mean absolutely nothing, happens on that ranch without your say-so.

A very serious job and a heavy responsibility, in other words, which not only requires courage and intelligence, but also a certain amount of dignity.

And something happens to a guy's dignity when he's brought to his knees by a BUG.

And to have this happen in front of one's True Love and Fondest Desire is a foolish crate.

A cruelish fate.

A cruel fate.

If you've ever been drilled by a flea, you'll understand. If you haven't, you can take my word for it: a drilling flea can take a grown dog to the mat and leave his dignity in scrambles. Real quick.

Okay. I hit the deck, so to speak, and launched my posse of teeth and went after that sneaking, overbearing little pipsqueak of a flea.

It might surprise you to know that dogs — even your higher bred blue-ribbon top-of-line cowdogs — have places on their bodies that cannot be defended against drilling fleas. It's true. A flea that strikes near the base of the tail cannot be stopped by ordinary means.

I had to go to extraordinary measures to combat this dog-eating flea. "Excuse me just one moment, Beulah, I have this . . . "

After running in circles and chasing my hiney for several seconds, I realized that I would have to change tactics. *That microscopic flea was armed with a six-foot drill bit, fellers, and he was doing incredible damage to my body!*

You're probably thinking that the cause was lost, that the alleged flea had succeeded in running his eight-foot tempered steel diamond-tipped gigantic drill bit through the entire length of my body, causing my precious fluids and liquids to leak out on the ground.

Is that what you thought? Well, you're in for a big surprise. As the old saying goes, "It's always darkest before it gets any darker."

What that flea didn't know about cowdogs was that when Emergency Defense System One fails, we don't quit. We initiate Emergency Defense System Two and go right on fighting!

We have our tricks, sec. Many tricks. Tricks that no flea has ever thought of.

Okay. You've got a flea drilling you from behind. You've launched several waves of tooth posses and they've been repealed. Repelled. And it appears that the situation is hopeless. You've been struck a deadly blow in a bodily zone that cannot be defended by conventional means.

So here's what you do. You sit down and lift both hind legs off the ground and raise them to a 45 degree angle. This concentrates all the weight of your body upon a small area near the base of your tail — which just happens to be the same small area where the pain, the terrible pain, is centered.

With the weight of your body concentrated over the area of pain and misery, you are ready to begin the most difficult part of the procedure. Pay close attention because I'll go over it only once.

G. L. Holmes

Back legs up, tail down, weight on back end. Now, *scoot forward, using front legs to pull rest of body around in a small circle, some 3-4 feet in diameter.* Repeat the procedure two or three times, as necessary.

I'll admit that, to an outside observer, a dog going through this procedure might appear a little silly. And it might have looked even sillier because, while I was attacking the flea problem, Mister Spasms-of-the-Heart was still rolling around on the ground.

But silly or not, my procedure worked, and nothing works better than something that works.

Okay. At last I had conquered the flea problem and rubbed him off the face of the earth, the hateful little snot, and was ready to turn my full attention back to the Department of Love.

I jumped to my feet, gave myself a good shake, and threw my gaze back to the pickup bed.

"Excuse the little diversion, Miss Beulah, but I'm sure you can . . . "

HUH?

Bird dog? A spotted bird dog?

That made no sense at all. Miss Beulah was a collie, not a . . . oh, it was HIM. Plato the Spotted Dumb-Bunny Bird Dog.

And he was laughing.

"By golly, Hank, that was one of the funniest routines I've seen in years!"

"Is that so?"

"Right. It was terrific! I don't know where you keep coming up with your material."

"It's pretty awesome, I guess."

"Right, it sure is, and Beulah loved it! I mean, she just loved it. I haven't seen her laugh so hard in years. Why, she's flat out on the floor right now."

"Isn't that wonderful."

"By golly, yes! You have a tremendous sense of comedy, Hank, and I mean that sincerely."

"Yeah? Well, you're fixing to see the second act."

I had already made up my mind to leap into the back of the pickup and show the bird dog the rest of my "routine," which would consist of me doing incredible damage to his face.

But just then Billy came out of the house. He waved goodbye to Slim, jumped into the pickup, and drove away.

Just before they disappeared into the storm, Plato yelled, "Terrific job, Hank, really terrific! It'll be a long time before Beulah and I forget this night!"

"Same here, Bird Dog, and that should cause you to lose a lot of sleep!"

And with that, they vanished into the night, leaving me alone with a huge crater in my heart.

And tail.

CHAPTER
6

A SICK BABY

T he world's best cure for a broken heart has always been a nice juicy bone. The next-best cure is a good night's sleep in front of a woodstove.

I had no juicy bones to help me through this dark and difficult period, and so when Slim came to the door and called us dogs into the house, I rushed inside and took my spot in front of the stove.

I still didn't think that a ranch dog had any business . . . I did it for medical reasons. A guy has to take care of his heart.

Did it work? Well, I managed to survive the night, even though I spent a large portion of my sleep time dreaming about a certain collie dog whose name I won't mention.

And listening to Drover's wheezing and grunting.

The next morning at daylight, I was awakened by the ringing of a bell. Not one to be fooled twice in a row, I suspicioned that it was the telephone and didn't bother to bark at it.

Okay, I barked at it a couple of times, but I was still asleep when I did it, so technically speaking, I wasn't actually fooled.

I heard Slim's feet hit the floor in the back bedroom. I heard him running down the hall. Then . . . his scratchy voice.

"Hello. No, I've been up for hours. Who is this? Oh, Loper. Morning. What time is it? I'll be derned. It is?"

Slim parted the curtains and looked out the window. "By gollies, it sure is. Looks like we might be in for a storm. The baby's sick? Say, that's no good. I guess the roads are too bad to . . . Cough medicine? Yeah, I've got a bottle of it somewhere. What? Speak up, Loper, I can't hardly hear you!

"No, you stay put. I'll try to make it in the flatbed. Oh, it ain't snowing that hard." He peeked out the window again. "It is snowing pretty hard, ain't it? But I'll make it, don't worry. See you in twenty minutes."

He hung up the phone and stretched his eyelids to get them open. "Little Molly's got a bad cough, dogs, and we've got to take some medicine up to her. I'd better find the derned stuff right now, else I'll run off and forget it, and wouldn't that be cute?"

He shuffled into the bathroom. Bottles clinked. He came out again, yawning and holding a bottle of something up close to his face. "Cough medicine, that's what it says. Okay, so far, so good."

He came over to the front of the stove and opened it up. "Move, dog, unless you want to go into the firebox."

On this ranch, manners don't get much exercise in the morning. The cowboys just grunt at you and threaten to throw you into the fire if you don't . . . oh well.

I moved.

He pitched in some crumpled-up newspapers and sticks of kindling, blew on the coals until the paper popped into flames, and then he added some chunks of fence-post cedar.

He'd slept in his one-piece red long-john underwear and left his jeans and shirt draped over the back of a chair, so it didn't take him long to get dressed.

He went out into the kitchen and flipped on the light switch. Nothing happened. The electric was still out because of the storm. He grumbled about that and made himself a quick breakfast: a cup of cold day-old coffee and a peanut-butter sandwich.

He dug his sheeplined coat and five-buckle galoshes out of the closet, put on his warmest gloves and his wool cap with the ear flappers, and headed for the door.

He slipped the bottle of medicine into the pocket of his sheepline and turned to us. "Come on, dogs, we've got work to do."

If I'd had a couple of minutes, I probably could have thought of a few things I'd rather do than go out into that cold blowing snow. I mean, it was pretty nasty outside, and there was never any question about whether or not we dogs would ride in the back of the pickup.

We rode in the cab with Slim.

We hadn't gone more than fifty yards down the road before we hit a deep drift. Slim had to get out out and lock in the front hubs, and then we started out again in four-wheel drive. The county road up to Loper's place had already begun to drift over. The wind was blowing hard, straight out of the north, and we couldn't see much of anything.

Slim had to hold his head at an angle to see out the windshield. "Boys, this storm is worse than I thought. I can't find the road. If I'd a-known it was blowing this hard . . . boys, I've got a feeling that we ain't going to make it."

All at once the pickup seemed to be sliding downward and tilting sideways, and Drover and I were sitting in Slim's lap, so to speak.

He shifted gears and gunned the motor, but we didn't move.

"Well, I've done it now," he said. "We're off in the ditch and this is the end of the line. And Hank, you stink!"

G.L. Holmes

He pushed me away and tried to open his door, but it was wedged against a snowdrift. He opened the door on the right side, pitched us out into the deep snow, and crawled out behind us.

Say, being out in that storm was a little bit scary. I mean, you couldn't see more than 25 feet in any direction and the wind was blowing so hard that it took your breath away.

For the first time, I noticed lines of fear on Slim's face. "Dogs, we have got ourselves in some trouble. If we can't find our way back to the house, we could be crowbait."

That's all it took to send Drover into a nervous breakthrough. "Oh Hank, I don't want to be crowbait and I'm too young to be a widow, and I'm so cold I just don't think I can make it and . . . oh, my leg!"

"Come on, dogs," Slim said, "stay close to me and don't get lost. We'll foller the barbed-wire fence as far as she goes, and then we'll have to strike out and walk into the storm — and hope we can find the house."

He waded and stumbled through the snow that had drifted into the ditch, and climbed up the bank on the other side until he reached the fence. He turned the collar of his sheepline up against the wind and started walking east, holding the top wire in his left hand.

Drover and I followed. I mean, Slim didn't need to worry about ME sticking close to him. All of a sudden that storm had made me feel pretty small and insignificant, which ain't exactly a normal feeling for your Heads of Ranch Security.

The snow was so deep, I couldn't walk in it, had to hop from one spot to the next. It was even harder for Mister Squeakbox, since his legs were only half as short as mine. Or half as long, I guess you could say.

Anyways, he was sawed-off at the legs. He'd try to walk on the top crust of the snow, don't you see, and that would work for a while, but then he'd break through and disappear.

It was tough going for him, and since Drover has never been one to suffer in silence, I got to hear all about it: he was freezing, he was tired, his nose was cold, his ears were cold, he was going snowblind, he'd lost the feeling in his stub tail, and his leg hurt, of course.

I got tired of hearing it. "Drover, dry up, will you?"

"I want to go to the machine shed!"

"Fine. Go to the machine shed, if you can find it."

"I wouldn't know where to look."

"Then dry up and walk."

"My legs are too short to walk in this snow!"

"Then fly."

"I can't fly!"

"Then shut your trap."

"Oh, my leg!"

It seemed to take us an hour to slog our way to the cattle guard, where the road turned north and went to Slim's place. Slim stopped and leaned against the corner post and fought for his breath.

I knew he was tired. I was tired too. Wading through that deep snow was a killer.

He caught his breath and knealt down. "Hank, come here, boy. My house lays a quarter-mile north of here. We won't have a fence to foller. Can you find the house?"

He had brought his face right down close to mine, and for some reason I felt an urge to give him a nice big juicy lick. Those urges sometimes strike me at odd moments, don't you see, and my tongue just shoots out before I have a chance to think about it.

And that's what it did — shot out and gave him a big slurpy lick on the face.

He spit and wiped his mouth. "Don't lick me, you doe-doe. Can you find the house in this storm?"

I glanced off to the north and saw . . . hmmm, a solid wall of white. No house. No road. No landmarks. No nuthin'. In other words . . .

I turned my eyes back to Slim's face. He looked pretty serious about this deal. I whapped my tail in the snow and tried to get the message across that, if our safety and survival depended on ME finding the house in that howling blizzard, we were probably in *real trouble.*

But he didn't wait for my message. He raised up, gave me a boot in the tail section, and said, "Find the house, pup, and don't spare the horses. I'm fadin' fast."

GULK.

ME? Find the . . . boy, this was no time for a miscalculation, I mean, if a guy happened to lose his bearings and head off in the wrong . . . surely I wasn't the best choice for this . . . perhaps if we postponed it until a nicer . . .

On the other hand, the awful responsibility of saving our little group seemed to have been thrust upon me. I got that impression when Slim booted me a second time and pointed his finger and entire arm towards the north.

"Find the house, Hank! Find the house!"

And so, with my heart pounding in my ears, I turned my nose into the howling wind and began walking into the terrible white nothingness before me.

CHAPTER
7

WHO, ME?

I hadn't gone more than ten steps when I realized that I was totally lost and without any sense of direction.

Facing that terrible wind, I couldn't see anything, and I will admit right here and for the record that I began to feel a certain uneasiness. Call it panic, if you will.

Scared silly.

Terrified.

I had just about decided to throw the Towel of Life into the Ring of . . . something. Into the Ring of Fate. I had just about decided to give up the struggle when, all at once, my nose picked up a scent in the snow.

I can tell you that there aren't too many scents in a snowstorm. Snow covers up most of your scents, don't you see, and that makes it tough on a dog, because under normal conditions we rely pretty heavily on our noses.

When that nose blanks out, fellers, it throws our whole navigation system out of whack.

Okay. I happened to lower my nose to a point just a few inches above the snow — and I began getting a reading! I walked a few steps further to the north and picked up another one.

Now, if you're familiar with the navigation business, you know that one reading isn't worth much because it's impossible to draw a straight line between one point.

It takes two points to make a line, see, and once I got the second reading, I knew that I was onto something. I had the two points I needed, and a line that pointed somewhere besides Oblivion.

I went several more steps and ran another check, and sure enough, there was Point Number Three!

Even though the road was buried under the snow, I knew that I was following it. Following the road, that is, not the snow. Well, I was following the snow too, but . . . forget it.

I had found a scent that would lead me straight to Slim's house!

You want to guess what it was? You'll probably guess that it was a trail of gasoline that had leaked out of the flatbed pickup.

Nice try. The flatbed leaked gas, all right, and oil

too, but the scent of gasoline doesn't last long. It evaporizes in the air.

No sir, the scent I had picked up came from *the tires of Billy's pickup* — which, if you recall, I had very carefully marked the night before.

Which just goes to prove how important it is for a dog to mark every tire of every vehicle that comes onto the ranch. A guy never knows when one of those routine marking jobs might save his life.

Well, once I had discovered my own mark in the snow, finding the house became a simple matter of switching over to instruments and running periodic checks of the navcom system. A piece of cake, in other words. No problem.

In fact, the only problem came when I got so far out in the lead, Slim had to call me back several times. Shucks, I was ready to take 'er on home and curl up in front of that stove!

When old Slim saw the house looming up ahead in the blizzard, he gave a cowboy yell and screeched, "You did it, Hankie! By gollies, you found the house!"

Well, what did he expect? I mean, you put the Head of Ranch Security in charge of things and you start seeing results, right?

I was the first to reach the house. I ran straight to the door and laid a mark on it, just to establish the fact that I had personally led a brave team of explorers through snow and ice and howling winds and conditions that weren't fit for man nor beets, and now I was planting our flag, so to speak, on the summit of the threshhold.

Slim arrived next, huffing steam in the air, his cheeks rosy red from the cold, his beard covered with frost, and his glasses fogged over.

Last, and definitely least, came Little Mister Squeak Box. "Oh Hank, I'm so cold, and this leg of mine . . ." And so forth.

Slim opened the door and we all staggered inside. Drover and I made a dash for the stove, while Slim stripped down to his red long-johns and his socks, and collapsed into his easy chair.

"Whew! Dogs, I don't know about you, but I am wore out. That's a terrible storm out there, as bad as any blizzard I ever saw. We're lucky we made it back to the house."

(I should point out that luck had nothing to do with it.)

Just then, the phone rang. Slim scowled at it. "Well, there's Loper, wondering what happened to us." He picked it up. "Hello? Hello? Can't hardly hear you, Loper. Something must be iced over, either the string or the tin cans."

He told Loper about our experiences in the blizzard — including the part about me guiding the expedition to the house.

"So we're afoot. I'm sure sorry, but man alive, I

couldn't find the dadgummed road! It's bad out there. Well, how's Molly doing?"

I studied his face. He pressed his lips together and shook his head.

"Well, that settles it. I'll start out afoot. Huh? No, I told you I'd get up there with the medicine, and that's what I'm a-going to do. Don't worry, I'll make it."

He hung up the phone and stared at us for a long time. "Boys, the thought of going back out in that storm kind of shakes me up, and I ain't scared of anything."

He stood up and started pulling on his clothes. The phone rang.

"Hello. Who is this? Oh. Speak up, Loper, can't hear you. Yes, you're right about that. Well, sure, it's risky but . . . Yes, he did, he sure did. I was right proud of the old . . . "

Slim's face rose into a big smile, and suddenly he was looking directly at me. I held my head up high and thumped my tail on the floor. By George, old Slim was sure . . .

"You know, that just might work! Tie the bottle around his neck and send him down the road!"

HUH?

Whoa, wait a minute, hold it, halt!

Tie the bottle around HIS neck and send HIM down the road?

Who was the HIM to be sent down the road, and WHOSE neck was being volunteered for WHAT?

"By gollies, Loper, I believe that's the best idea of the year. I'll get him on his way." He hung up the phone and flashed a big grin and took a step in my direction. "Here, Hankie, come here, boy."

Oh yeah? "Here, Hankie" my foot! If old Slim thought that THIS Hankie was going to . . . no way was he going to pitch me out into . . . there must have been some mistake, because surely . . .

I, uh, went into Stealthy Retreat Mode and, uh, began slinking back towards the, uh, bedroom, so to speak, while casting glances back towards Slim to see if he, uh, had any crazy notions about, well, following me.

He did seem to have such notions, and yes, he was following me.

"Come here, Hankie, I've got a little job for you."

He came at a slow walk. I moved away at a slow walk. He picked up the pace. I picked up the pace. He made a dash for me and I made a dash for the back of the house.

"Hank, come back here!"

Come back here? Was he losing his mind? What kind of fool did he think he was dealing with?

Hey, I might appear dumb on a few rare occasions, but when the chips are down, and when they're MY chips, fellers, I don't just stand around looking simple.

I run and hide under the nearest bed!

I went streaking down the hall and slithered my way under the bed — fighting my way through all the cobwebs and dust and lint that had accumulated there. "Jenny wool," we call it.

I saw Slim's nose appear under the bed, then his eyes. He was wearing a crazy grin on his mouth.

"Hi, puppy. I see you."

Yeah, well, he could look at me all he wanted, but as far as me coming out . . . no sale.

"Hank, get out from under that bed!"

No way, Charlie.

"I'll get the broom."

So get the broom.

He got the broom. He swept and he swatted, and I could have told him that no broom was going to flush me out from under that bed.

At last he gave up on the broom. His face appeared again. It didn't look so friendly this time.

"Hank, I've got this great opportunity for you."

Yes, I knew all about his "great opportunity."

"And I'm giving you one last chance to volunteer. And if you don't come out from under that bed, I'm a-going to pull off the mattress and springs and kick your little doggie butt up between your shoulder blades."

I took a deep breath and thought the deal over one last time. Slim needed help. The baby needed

G.l. Holmes

the medicine. Duty was calling. I was the best dog
for the job.

Ah, what the heck, maybe I could . . . I crawled
out from under the bed and volunteered for the job.

Yes, I knew it was going to be one of the most
dangerous missions of my entire career. I knew there
was a chance that I would never reach my destination,
that I might be lost in the raging storm and never
heard from again.

I knew all that. But I also understood the terrible
consequences that might occur if I didn't go.

I might become a permanent freak. I would be laughed at and scorned. I would never win the heart of another woman.

Girl-dogs will forgive many flaws, but they aren't impressed by guys who wear their fannies up around their shoulder blades.

CHAPTER
8

DON'T FORGET:
I VOLUNTEERED

S lim carried me into the bathroom and closed the
door behind us.

That really wasn't necessary. Did he actually think
that I might... hey, I had *volunteered* for this mission!
He didn't need to treat me like a common crinimal.

I resented that. It really hurt.

On the other hand, I did happen to notice that he
had left a little crack in the door, and I wondered
what might happen if I hooked my paw around...

SLAM!

He couldn't take a joke, that's all. No sense of
humor.

He left me alone in that prison cell and returned
a few minutes later. He was holding an old boot top
that had been stitched at one end so that it would
hold cow medicine.

He shoved the bottle of cough medicine inside the boot top, rigged up a kind of harness device out of whang leather, and tied it around my neck.

This deal showed every indication of getting out of hand. I mean, it appeared that he might actually go through with it.

He left the room again, and when he came back, I was sorry to see that he was dressed for cold weather. The worm of fate had crawled another step towards the apple of . . . something.

Disaster, probably.

"Well, Hankie, all these years we've been a-saying that you ain't worth eight eggs. I guess this is your big opportunity to prove us wrong. Or maybe right. You ready?"

You bet I was ready — so ready that I tried my very best to crawl into the cabinet where he kept his towels and wash rags. He grabbed me and I sank my claws into the nearest towel and went to digging.

He got me out of there, but he knew he'd been in a struggle. And I carried one of those towels all the way to the front door.

As we passed Drover, he raised his head and gave me a grin. "Good old Hank, what a guy! I'd sure like to go with you, but this old leg of mine . . . "

I wasn't able to come up with words to express the thoughts that marched across the vast expanse of my mind. So I just glared at him and hoped that the cruel slant of my eyes would convey the message.

Suddenly we were outside in the raging ferocious blizzard. I could hear the wind roaring like a freight train through the cottonwoods. Frozen limbs creaked. The snow swirled before my snow-blinded eyes. I gasped for breath.

Surely Slim wouldn't . . . it was time for Heavy Begs. I moaned and whined and tried to kick my legs. No luck.

Slim didn't put me down at this point, which struck me as a shabby cheap trick and a vote of no confidence. I mean, did he think I would try to scramble back into the house or hide behind the wood pile or make a run for the feed barn?

Yes, apparently that's what he thought, and come to think of it . . . but I didn't get the opportunity because he carried me away from the house, out into the storm, and down the road, which wasn't there any more because it was buried under six inches of snow.

Oh yes, and along the way he pulled a limb off a tree and I couldn't imagine what he might . . .

At last he stopped and dropped me into the snow. It would be hard for me to express just how awful that snow felt as it closed around my nice warm paws and invaded the inner warmth of my inner being.

Let's just say that it felt awful, and that I looked up into his eyes and switched my tail over to the

G. L. Holmes

I-Don't-Believe-You're-Doing-This-To-A-Loyal-Friend Mode.

That didn't work either.

"Go home, Hank. Take the medicine to Molly. Double dog food if you make it."

Oh yeah? And what if I didn't make it? It would be double dog food for the buzzards, right?

"Go on! Go to the house. Find Loper."

I whimpered and moaned and howled and cried and tried to . . . but he raised his stick in a threatening manner, almost as though he planned to . . .

"GO HOME!"

Okay, all right. I just hadn't understood his . . . he wanted me to find my way back to the house, it appeared, and perform a very dangerous mission of mercy, which was sort of my specialty, and there was no need to yell and threaten and . . .

GULP.

It seemed that heroism had been thrust upon me, and as I've said many times before, when all else fails, a guy might as well go ahead and do what's good and right.

Yes, they had definitely chosen the right dog for this job. Or, to put it another way, they were very lucky that I had volunteered for this mission.

I glanced up into Slim's face one last time, just in case he might have thought it over and changed his . . . drawing back the stick? That was uncalled for, I mean, it's not necessary to bully and browbeat the Head of Ranch . . .

"Go home, Hank, go home!"

All at once I felt a powerful urge to go home. Yes, and to deliver the precious healing medicine that

G.L.Holmes

would cure Baby Molly of the cough that had tormented her sleep.

The words of my Cowdog Oath returned to me: ". . . to protect and defend all innocent children against all manner of monsters and evil things, regardless of the consequences."

And with those words fresh in my mind, I turned my back on the comfort of the house and the warmth of the stove (Drover would pay for this) and went plunging into the Great White Unknown.

The tracks we had left in the snow half an hour before had already vanished, but I had no trouble finding my way back to the cattle guard. That was the easy part — traveling with the wind at my back and following my own scent in the snow.

I reached the cattle guard in good shape and in record time. But once I had conquered the easy part, the part that remained to be conquered promised to be less than easy.

Hard.

Very difficult.

Somewhere between impossible and ridiculous.

At the cattle guard, I negotiated a 90 degree turn into a crosswind that was running about 40 degrees below zero, and began stumbling through snow that had drifted much deeper than I might have wished.

This was tough going, fellers. I mean, every step in that deep snow required a terrible effort, and after fifteen or twenty of those lunging steps, I was already shot.

But I couldn't stop. The words of my Cowdog Oath kept me going. Also the knowledge that if I stopped, I would become a doggie Popsicle. I mushed on.

After what seemed hours, I reached the flatbed

pickup, which we had left abandoned in the ditch. The hood had already disappeared beneath a drift.

I paused for a moment to catch my breath, then plunged onward into the storm. I reached the top of that hill just south of the alfalfa field. So far, so good. But the last mile to the house would be the most treacherous, for there were no trees or haystacks or fences or other landmarks to mark the land.

Up ahead, I saw nothing but a huge white blank. Up until recently, it had been my policy to avoid huge white blanks, but there appeared to be no way of avoiding this one.

Gulp.

I decided that my best hope in this hopeless situation would be to leave the road — or what used to be the road — and follow the creek in a westerly direction. That would give me some protection from the wind and a trace to follow.

There was only one small risk in this approach. On our way down to Slim's place, we had seen several coyotes dash across the road. Where do you suppose a coyote would go if he got caught out in a blizzard?

To the low ground, to the creek bottom, to the shelter of trees and bluffs.

Fellers, the thought of bumping into a band of hungry cannibals didn't exactly warm my heart, but neither did the thought of getting lost in the blizzard.

So I stopped thinking about it and staggered down the hill towards the creek bottom. It was much better down there. The snow wasn't nearly as deep and I made good time, traveling right on the edge of the water where the snow had melted away.

Yes, this was fine. I increased my pace from a slow walk to a rapid walk, and then to a trot. I began calculating my Estimated Time of Arrival and figgered that if all went well, I would reach the house in about

. . .

HUH?

Rip and Snort? Blocking my path? Surely this was a tropical illusion, sometimes when you've been traveling for a long time through snow, you become snow-blind and your eyes begin playing . . .

Licking their chops?

Uh oh. Fellers, I had just blundered into the winter camp of a couple of dog-eating coyotes. That's not something you want to do when you're out on an important errand of mercy.

CHAPTER
9

SNOWBOUND
WITH CANNIBALS

I did a quick about-face and began marching in the other direction, hoping that the coyotes might think they had seen a mirage. Or something.

I had only gone three steps when I heard them shout, "Halt! Stop! Not try to escape!"

I, uh, pretended not to hear them. That can happen sometimes, when the wind's blowing hard. I hoped they'd understand, but just in case they didn't, I cast a glance over my . . . they were coming after me, plunging through the snow with big leaps.

"Halt! Not walk away when coyote say halt!"

I picked up my pace somewhat, moving into a rapid walk and then into a dog trot. When I sensed that this wasn't working, I reached for the afterburners and went to Escape Speed.

G.L. Holmes

And ran smack into them. Those guys were fast.

They weren't smiling, not at all. They looked very serious, almost angry. Angry. And hungry.

Snort narrowed his eyes and gave me a sniffing.

"That you, Hunk, with face covering up with many snowflake?"

"Me? With my face covered up with snowflakes? No, it's not me at all. There's been some mistake."

"Uh. Snort thinking we find ranch dog name Hunk."

"Oh no. No, no. No, not at all."

"You looking berry much like Hunk, Snort think, and Rip too."

Rip nodded his head, and they continued to stare at me with their yellow eyes.

"No, I think this is just a simple case of mistaken identity, Snort. I'm not me at all. That is, I'm not who you think I am, unless . . . eh, just out of curiosity, what do you think of this 'Hunk' feller? Tell me about him."

"Chicken dog."

"No, that's not me."

"Dummy ranch dog."

"See? You've got the wrong guy, and I really . . . "

Snort blocked my path. "Hunk all the time making coyote look foolish, play many trick."

"No! You mean, there's a dog around here who could make *you guys* look foolish? I can hardly believe that."

"Better you believe that."

"Right. I believe that with all my heart and soul and liver and . . . "

"Coyote hungry for liver."

"I didn't say liver. I said 'heart and soul.'"

"Uh. Coyote hungry for heart."

"I didn't say heart. I must have misquoted you, so let me run the whole thing past you again. I said, 'I believe that will hardly deliver my soul,' is exactly what I said, word for word. Honest."

"Uh."

"Nothing about hearts or livers."

"Not make sense, 'hardly deliver soul.'"

"You're right, Snort, so let's just scratch out the business about the soul. That leaves us with, 'I believe that will hardly deliver the mole.' How does that grab you?"

"Ha! Mole not grab coyote. Coyote grab mole and swallow in two bites, yum yum."

"Now we're getting somewhere! What you guys need is a nice fat mole to eat, and I'll bet that if you'd stick your heads into that big snowdrift over there and count to five thousand, you'd find one. No kidding, I really think you'd . . . "

"You wipe snow off of face."

"Say what? Wipe snow off of . . . "

Rip stepped forward and slugged me under the chin, causing my head to fly back and red checkers to form behind my eyes, and sending the snow flying off of my face.

And all at once I was exposed, stripped of my disguise in front of two of the most dreadful cannibals in Ochiltree County.

They gave me big toothy grins. "Ah ha, Hunk hiding behind snow!"

"No, wait a minute. I wasn't exactly . . . "

"And now Hunk captured."

"Captured? Well, surely we can . . . " I glanced around and checked out the escape routes. The coyote brothers filled them.

"Hunk not try run away."

"Oh no, I wouldn't think of . . . "

"Hunk stay for supper."

"Thanks, Snort, but I really ought to . . . "

"Because Hunk MAKE supper for hungry brothers, ha ha."

"That's not funny, Snort. You ought to be ashamed of yourself, laughing at the misfortunes of others."

He stuck his nose right in my face. "Rip and Snort tear up whole world and spit, not feel ashamed for nothing."

"Okay, let's try another approach. You see this thing around my neck? It's medicine for a sick child — a little baby girl-child who has a terrible cough."

"Coyote not give hoot for terrible cough."

"I haven't finished yet, Snort, and I'd appreciate it if you'd suspend judgment until I'm done."

"Coyote not give hoot for suspender juggling."

"Of course you do. See, you probably didn't realize that I'm on an errand of mercy."

"Coyote not give hoot for arrow of mercy."

I glared at them. "Rip, Snort, I must tell you that I'm shocked and dismayed. I've never encountered such closed minds and cold hearts."

"Uh! Coyote hungry for heart."

"Forget I said that, I'm sorry I mentioned it. The point is that I'm shocked and dismayed."

"Ha! Coyote not give hoot for chock full of dismay."

"Okay." My mind was racing. I had to come up with something, real quick. "Let's try another approach: singing."

Their ears shot up and their yellow eyes began to sparkle. "Uh! Coyote give BIG hoot for singing! Rip and Snort berry greater singest in whole world, oh boy."

"I doubt that, Snort. You guys might be . . . "

Snort poked me in the chest with his paw and curled his lip just enough to expose two rows of incredible fangs. "Hunk not bad-talk coyote music! Rip and Snort berry greater singest in whole big world!"

"Yes, well, I hope you didn't think I . . . what I'm saying, guys, is that you might be great singers . . . "

"Not might. Greater singest for sure!"

"All right, for sure, but you haven't heard my latest love song."

Rip rolled his eyes. "Uh."

"But I can already tell that you're dying to hear it."

Snort shook his head. "Not dying."

"All right. You're not dying to hear it, but you're very anxious to hear my latest love song."

"Coyote rather eat than hearing love song. Coyote not give hoot for love."

"But this is a different kind of love song, Snort. It's about fleas."

He perked up on that. "Uh! Coyote got plenty fleas." He sat down in the snow and began scratching his ear with his hind leg. "Got flea right now, ha!"

"See there? I knew you'd like it. It's called, 'Oh Flee, My Love.'"

They were waiting for me to sing. I could tell that I had picked . . . perked . . . piqued . . . pricked their interest. Gotten their attention. Tapped into to their cultural level.

Snort stopped scratching and frowned at me. "So? Love song about flea okay with coyote. Hunk sing about loving flea."

"Well, I really hadn't come prepared . . . I didn't bring my music, don't you see, and . . . "

"HUNK SING!!"

"All right, all right, but remember that you forced me to do this."

And with that, I sang them my latest bombshell of a song.

Oh Flee, My Love!

I saw her face that snowy night and felt the love bug
crawl.

As melting snow dripped off my chin, I promised her
my all.

Or if not all, then some of it, the part that I could spare.

I offered her my heart's spare part, I promised it right
there.

Her eyes showed pure astonishment, I knew I'd done
the trick.

Her mouth turned up into a smile that would have
melted brick.

I knew I had her on the ropes, I knew I couldn't fail.

And that's when I became aware of something near
my tail.

At first I tried to let it slide, I figgered it was just

That same old crawling bug of love I'd noticed right at
first.

And so I winked my eye at her and gave her one more
thrill,

But suddenly that bug of love attacked me with a drill.

When something's drilling on your tail, it's hard to
keep your suave,

I lost my concentration then and knew I had to solve

The mystery of that piercing pain that had a hold of
me

The bug of love that bit so hard turned out to be a flea!

C H A P T E R
10

DEVOURED BY COYOTES

Well, I finished my song and turned to the coyote brothers. They were staring at me with dull brutish expressions on their dull brutish faces.

"What do you think, Snort?" No answer. "Would it surprise you to know that that song was based on a true life experience?" No answer. "It happened to me only last night. I'll bet you'd like to hear the whole story behind it, huh?" He yawned. "Okay, here we go. It all began last . . . "

"Coyote not caring for love or pretty music."

"Yeah, but all things considered, it's the kind of song that a coyote can really go for. I mean, it was so good, you're probably thinking about letting me go."

They got a big laugh out of that.

"Or maybe not. Which is just fine, as long as I don't have to listen to any of your lousy coyote songs."

That got their attention, which is what I had hoped might happen. I had run out of good ideas, see, and was stalling for time, in hopes of postponing supper.

Snort pushed himself up and came lumbering over to me. "What means, 'lousy coyote song?'"

"It means . . . well, I hate to put it this way, Snort, especially with your hot breath right in my face, could you back up a little bit? No? Okay, we'll just . . . I hate to say this, but I doubt that you guys have a song that's in the same class with 'Oh Flee, My Love.'"

"Uh. What's meaning 'class?'"

"Class is something you've never had, Snort, and probably never will. I mean, you guys only know one song, right?"

"Guys know two song."

"All right, two songs."

He counted three claws on his right foot. "Coyote know *seven* song."

"Wait a minute. You counted three claws. How could you come up with seven songs?"

He scowled and counted again. "One. Four. Seven. Coyote know seven song."

"No, no. You cheated, Snort. One claw plus one claw plus one claw makes *three* claws."

He stuck his nose in my face. "One claw plus one claw plus one claw make fat lip if dog not shut up."

"Oh, I see now. You're using Coyote Mathematics."

"Whatsomever."

"Which means that you count to three, multiply by two, and add one."

"Uh uh. Add *two*, not one."

"No, that would make eight." He whacked me on the nose. "No, by George, that would make seven."

"Ha! Hunk pretty smart."

"Yes sir, that Coyote Mathematics is pretty foxy stuff."

"Coyote not like fox."

"That's what I meant. It's not foxy at all."

"Coyote know seven song."

"That's certainly the bottom line, isn't it?"

"Uh."

"Which means that you've got a song or two I haven't heard, and I'll bet you're scared to sing in a blizzard."

"Ha! Coyote not scared of buzzard."

"Yeah, but I said blizzard."

"Coyote eat lizard in one bite. Not scared of lizard."

"No, you missed it again. I said . . . "

He poked me in the nose. "Hunk talk too much. Coyote not scared of nothing."

"All right, then sing your old song. I dare you to sing it right now, in the middle of a blinded snow . . . "

He shoved me down into a sitting position. "Hunk shut trap and listen."

"I can handle that."

"And after we singing, then we eat, oh boy!"
"I don't think I could hold another bite, Snort."
"Shut trap!"
"Yes sir."

I shut my trap and listened to their new song. It turned out to be another low-class musical experience, a little piece of coyote trash called "We Don't Give A Hoot."

We Don't Give a Hoot

I guess you might think we are dumb and stupid,
And maybe you think we can't sing.
And maybe you think we can't make up rhymes,
And if that's what you think . . .

Then we've got a message for you, mister,
And you'd better listen real good,
'Cause we've got one thing to say to you
And here is what it is . . .

We don't give a hoot,
We don't ever wear a suit.
We're nothing but animals,
Outrageous cannibals,
We don't give a hoot.

I guess you might think that we smell bad
But it's only because we stink.
But who wants to smell like petunias?

Not me . . .

Me and my brother don't want to offend
Anyone with our smell,
So if you should find us offensive,
We will beat you up . . .

'Cause we don't give a hoot,
We don't ever wear a suit.
We're nothing but animals,
Outrageous cannibals,
We don't give a hoot.

Being a cannibal's lots of fun and goofing off,
We don't ever have to take baths.
Or clean up our room or eat any spinach
Or dental floss our teeth . . .

We fight all the time and howl at the moon,
And pick our noses a lot.
And if you don't like what we're singing
We'll beat you up again . . .

'Cause we don't give a hoot,
We don't ever wear a suit.
We're nothing but animals,
Outrageous cannibals,
We don't give a hoot.

Well, when they finished their song, Snort

swaggered over to me. He was wearing a huge grin on his face and I could tell that he was proud of himself.

"Uh! What Hunk say now?"

"Well, uh, you might say that I'm at a loss for words . . . so to speak."

"Better find words real quick, so to speaking."

"Right. Well, Snort, on the one hand, that is a very, uh, strange song." He bared his fangs. "But on the other hand, it's strangely beautiful, in a strange sort of way."

"Not strange."

"Exactly. Not strange at all."

"Only beautiful."

"Right, you stole the words right out of my mouth."

"Ha! Coyote like to steal."

"Yes sir, you're quite a thief, Snort, and I say that from the bottom of my . . . "

Oops.

A gleam came into Snort's eyes. "Uh! Coyote hungry for heart!"

"I didn't say that word, honest, cross my heart . . . oops."

"Coyote not care what Hunk say. Coyote ready for big grub, oh boy!"

They were coming towards me, licking their chops.

"Now wait a second, let's don't . . . " I started backing up. "How about another song, guys? I mean, it would be a shame to quit just when we've . . . "

They were shaking their heads.

I kept backing up until my backside backed into an embackment. Embankment, that is. And there I stopped. I had reached a dead end and was surrounded by cannibals.

In the Security Business, we have developed many escape procedures for many difficult situations, but we have never solved the puzzle of how to escape a dog out of a dead-end situation, surrounded by cannibals.

That's a toughie. All reported cases have ended in sudden death, followed by feasting, singing, and loud belching.

In other words . . . I think you've got the picture. I was in BIG trouble.

Wouldn't it be a shame if I got eaten? Not only would that mess up my plans for the future, but it would just about ruin the story. And what about Little Molly and her cough? Had you stopped to think about that?

If the coyote brothers happened to eat me for supper, then it follows from simple logic that there would be nothing left of me to finish my errand of mercy in the howling blinded blizzard, or to deliver the medicine to Little Molly.

Just think about poor Little Molly. Coughing all night, crying, coughing some more. Can you see Sally

May standing over her crib, biting her lip and . . .

When I say "biting her lip," I mean that Sally May is biting Sally May's lip, not Molly's lip. She'd never do that. Sally May wouldn't bite her child's . . . never mind.

Anyways, can you see Sally May standing over the baby's lip and biting her crib? Her face shows the little web-lines of worry and she's wringing her hands.

Nearby, Loper is pacing the floor. "It's all resting on the shoulders of our Heroic Guard Dog."

"Yes," says Sally May. "He's such a wonderful dog!"

"But where could he be? Something terrible must have happened, hon, because . . . "

"I know. Because nothing but a catastrophe could have stopped Hank from bringing the medicine to our sick child."

"Yeah. What a dog!"

"He's so wonderful!"

"I only wish I had dozen dogs just like him."

"At least a dozen. Well . . . " She walks to the window and looks out at the swirling terrible frozen blizzard outside. "We can only pray that he makes it."

Pretty touching scene, huh? I can't tell you for sure that such a scene actually happened, but I'm guessing that it did. Or could have.

Yes, the terrible responsibility of making it through the storm and delivering the medicine to Little Molly was on my massive shoulders, and you're probably sitting on the edge of your chair right now, wondering what happened next, right?

Okay, hang on.

The coyotes ate me and that's the end of the story.

G.L. Holmes

I already told you, I got eaten by coyotes. You needn't bother to turn the page again.

CHAPTER
11

JUST KIDDING

Y ou turned the page again, didn't you?

And by now you've figgered out that I wasn't actually eaten alive by hungry cannibals and the story isn't over yet. But it MIGHT have turned out that way if . . .

You won't believe this. I didn't believe it either, but it happened. Okay, I was backed into a corner and surrounded by Rip and Snort, who werc all set to start supper. Things looked real bad for Yours Truly.

Well, all of a sudden a bird-like object poked its head out of a hole in the embankment. The bird-like object rescmbled, well, a bird, you might say. In fact, it was a bird.

An owl. A little owl.

HUH?

Holy smokes, it was Madame Moonshine, the witchy little owl! The soggy condition of her eyes suggested that she had just awakened from a nap.

"Excuse me," she yawned, "but by any chance, are you an owl?"

"An owl? No, I don't think so."

"How strange! I could have sworn that I heard an owl hooting."

"Oh, that. No, it was the coyote brothers, singing a song about how they don't give a hoot."

"My goodness. I thought that coyotes howled and owls hooted. Now you're telling me that coyotes hoot. I suppose the next thing you'll tell me is that owls howl."

"No, I don't think . . . hey Madame, I've got a small problem I need to discuss with you."

"Did you realize that owl + H = Howl? I find mathematical relationships so fascinating! Don't you? And speaking of you . . . " She blinked her eyes and stared at me. "My goodness! Unless I'm still dreaming, you are Hank the Rabbit."

"Hank the Cowdog, ma'am, Head of . . . "

"And shame on you for waking me up!"

"Let me get right to the point, Madame. These coyotes are fixing to eat me, and if you've got one trick left in your bag of tricks, I'd be mighty grateful if you'd pull it out, real quick."

She smiled. "Quick trick. Did you realize that Quick – Qu + Tr = Trick? Oh, these universal principles are just wonderful! Everything is related, you see, which means that we're all relatives."

"Madame, please hurry."

"But if all things are relative, then nothing is actually related. Oh, it's all so wonderful but so confusing!"

"Madame, those coyotes are planning to eat me."

"Coyotes? Oh yes, coyotes. Are these the same coyotes who hoot?"

"They're the same coyotes who don't GIVE a hoot."

"Oh, then I was mistaken. I thought you said they were some sort of hooting coyotes."

"Well, yes, they were hooting, but they were hooting about how they don't give a hoot."

She shook her head and sighed. "I'm confused. How can one hoot when one doesn't give a hoot?"

"Never mind the hoots, Madame, THEY'RE GOING TO EAT ME!"

"Oh rubbish! Surely they wouldn't . . . " She saw their fangs and drooling lips and sparkling yellow eyes. "My goodness. On second thought, I think you have a point. They do look threatening."

"Right. And when they're finished eating me, they're liable to be looking for a dessert with feathers on it."

All at once her eyes popped wide open. "I think we have just moved out of the realm of abstraction, Hank, and yes, we do need a trick — quick."

"Thank you, Madame, and please hurry."

She closed her eyes and concentrated. By this time, the coyote brotherhood had gotten close enough so that I was getting a much better look at their bloodshot eyes than I wanted.

"I've got it!" she said at last. "Timothy will save us." She stuck her head back into her cave and called, "Timothy? Timothy! Come here at once! We are under siege."

You remember Big Tim, Madame Moonshine's personal bodyguard? He was a great big huge nasty-looking six-foot diamondback rattlesnake, and boy, do I dislike great big huge snakes, and boy, did I have a hard time sitting still when he came crawling out of the cave and coiled up between me and Madame!

He flicked out his tongue at me, and in what I would describe as a weak voice, I managed to say, "Hey, Tim, how's it going, pardner?"

Because I'm scared of snakes, just don't like 'em at all. I mean, I don't allow rattlesnakes around headquarters and I've killed my share of 'em in the yard, but I'd never tangled with one even half as big as Timothy, and fellers, Timothy was pretty muchly free to come and go as he pleased on my ranch.

Biggest rattlesnake I'd ever seen, and hey, when
he flicked that tongue out at me, the thought of being
eaten by coyotes lost some of its sting, so to speak.

"Uh Madame, do you suppose you could point your
snake in the right direction? He's staring at ME, and

my ma always told me to be careful around loaded snakes."

"Oh rubbish, he wouldn't ... Timothy, you naughty snake, stop glaring at Hank! And stop sticking out your tongue at him! Shame on you! The enemy is over there."

She pointed a wing at the Coyote Brotherhood. Big Tim gave me one last glare — and I'm almost sure that he curled his lip at me too — and swung around to face the approaching barbarians.

That made me feel much better. I mean, my favorite rattlesnake pal was fixing to clean house on Rip and Snort, and I was all set to enjoy the show.

Madame stood erect and addressed the brothers. "Excuse me? My name is Madame Moonshine, and this is my cave. I have a few words to speak to you."

The brothers stopped and grinned at each other. Madame went on with her speech.

"I'm sorry to tell you this, but I do not allow ruffians near my cave. Now, shoo and scat!" They didn't move. "I shall say it one more time: shoo and scat!" They didn't move. "Very well, you leave me no choice. Unless you leave at once, I shall have to resort to drastic measures."

They just sat there, staring and grinning. Madame continued.

"I perceive that you're not familiar with the different species of serpent, so let me warn you that

Timothy is a registered Skull-and-Crossbones Turbo-Diamondback Rattlesnake. He is trained to attack. His venom has been tested and certified by the Bureau of Terrible Things.

"He is armed with two .9MM Uzi fully automatic fangs, with silencers and infrared detection devices, which enable him to perform his duties in total darkness. He is capable of striking a target in .13858 seconds, and," she smiled, "we have never had the opportunity to time him on a second strike. We keep losing our targets after one shot."

She patted him on the head and turned back to the coyotes.

"And now, you may leave. I wish you a happy snow storm and a good day."

The brothers didn't leave. What they did kind of surprised me. They started laughing. They fell over on their backs and rolled in the snow and kicked their legs in the air, yipped and hollered and hooted and howled, got a heck of a big laugh out of Madame's speech.

Hey, I had always suspected that those guys were a couple of bales short of a full load of brains, but laughing at Big Tim set a new record for Dumb.

Snort jumped to his feet and shook the snow off his coat. "Uh! Coyote ready for play with snake."

"Does that mean you won't be leaving?"

"Uh! Send snake for big fun in snow."

"Very well, you have been warned." Madame Moonshine swiveled her head around to Big Tim. "Timothy, go teach the ruffians a lesson. Charge! Talleyho!"

Tim zipped his head around and glared me again. "Don't point that thing at me, you . . . uh, Mister Timothy. In other words, please go get the coyotes . . . if you please, that is."

He stuck out his tongue at me one last time — I told you he couldn't be trusted — and he went slithering out to rout the barbarian hoards.

I couldn't help admiring the way that snake moved. I mean, not only was he huge, but he was also quick. I figgered it wouldn't take old Timothy long to . . .

You know, I'd almost forgotten just how tough Rip and Snort were. I've said before that they loved a good brawl above all other things, even eating, and they were no more afraid of that snake than if he'd been a big worm.

You know what they did? While Tim hissed and coiled and struck and put on a demonstration of his Oozie-Turbo-Whatever-It-Was, Rip and Snort simply dodged and weaved and kept out of his fangs — laughing and hooting all the while.

And then do you know what they did? When old Tim ran out of Turbo, Snort picked him in his jaws and pitched him to Rip, and I'll just be derned if they didn't play pass-and-touch right there in the midst of

the blizzard — using Timothy the Turbo-Worm as their football!

I had suspected all along that Timothy was just a big windbag. He sure hadn't impressed me much.

Well, I looked at Madame Moonshine and she looked at me. She was the first to speak. "They're playing football with my bodyguard."

"Yes, and having a pretty good time, I'd say. Did you have any other ideas for getting us out of this mess?"

"I'm afraid not. Unless . . . " She stared at me with her big owlish eyes. "Is there any reason why we're sitting here, watching this disgraceful folly, when we could probably pick up and leave?"

I shot a glance at the brothers. Snort was running a deep post pattern and Rip was winding up to throw the bomb. They were moving farther and farther away from us.

"No, by George, in his own peculiar way, old Timothy just might have saved our bacon. On the other hand, his own bacon seems to be up for grabs, so to speak."

She sniffed at that. "Timothy will survive. Whether or not he will keep his job is another question. I had expected dramatic results, but of a different sort. Shall we go?"

"Yes, let's."

And with that, we turned to the west and went streaking up the creek.

Don't forget, I still had an important mission to accomplish.

C H A P T E R
12

A BY-GEORGE
HAPPY, HEROIC ENDING

Well, I had somehow managed to dodge another
bullet — with a small assist from Madame
Moonshine and her phoney wind-bag snake — and
now it was time to get back to business.

Madame and I went plunging into the eye of the
teeth of the storm, and soon we disappeared behind
the curtain of snow. Shortly after the curtain of snow
dropped behind us, I began to suspect that I had lost
my axles. Bearings.

"Madame," I yelled over the wind, "which way is
west?"

"Just look for the setting sun."

"The sun isn't setting, and even if it were, we
wouldn't be able to see it for all the snow."

"That's true, and oh dear. It appears that we are lost in the storm."

"Great."

"Unless . . . "

"Tell me more about *unless*."

"Well, I do have these magical sensory powers, but using them requires a great deal of effort. And if I help you find your way back to the ranch house, you won't be able to keep me company throughout the rest of the storm."

I explained to her just how important this mission was — you know, about the sick baby and so forth.

She sighed. "Very well, I suppose I can try."

She hopped herself up on my back and directed my nose in what I hoped was the right direction, although it seemed all wrong to me.

I went charging through the snow and wind. The minutes passed. I was getting tired. I'd been out in that terrible storm for several hours, you know, and traveling through that deep snow was beginning to wear me down.

On and on we went, until at last I had to stop and catch my breath. "Madame, I just hit the bottom of my breakfast. I don't think I can go another step. I guess we're lost."

"Yes, and I feel terrible about it. You trusted me, didn't you, Hank?"

"I guess I did, yes."

"On the other hand, what is that object directly to our right?"

I turned my head and squinted into the snow. "Well, let's see. It looks a little bit like a . . . hmmmm, a yard gate covered with snow."

"My goodness, a yard gate? If there is a yard gate, then do you suppose there might be a yard to go with it? And where you find a yard, you often find a house nearby."

All at once the pieces of the puzzle were beginning to fall into place. "By George, Madame, I believe we've found our way back to the . . . Madame? Madame Moonshine?"

She had vanished. One second she had been sitting on my back, and the next, she was gone, and hadn't even bothered to say goodbye, almost as though she had, well, planned it that way.

Hmmm. That was a very strange little owl, but you might say that I didn't take the time to think about it, because right then my most important job was to bark at the house and finish my job.

Using the very last of my energy reserves, I waded through a deep drift and collapsed on the porch. I wasn't sure that I had enough energy to scratch on the door. I mean, I was beat, wiped out.

Exhausted.

On Death's doormat.

Going into convulsions of tiredness.

Frostbitten and snow-blinded and hypothermiated. No ordinary dog could have . . .

"Mmmmmm, hello, Hankie. Been out for a little walk in the snow?"

My ears twitched. Throwing the very last of my energy reserves into the task, I raised one eyelid. And there, curled up in a little ball on the porch, was Pete the Barncat.

He was smirking at me. "I was here first, Hankie, and this is my porch."

Throwing the very last of my energy reserves into the task, I opened my other eye and staggered to my feet. "Oh yeah?"

"Um hmm. First come, first served."

Funny, I was feeling stronger by the second. "Oh yeah?"

"Um hmmm. And if you don't leave my porch right now, I'll screech and yowl and cry and limp around in circles, and guess who will come outside with her broom."

"Oh yeah?"

"That's right, Hankie. Sally May will come out with her broom and . . . "

"ROOOOF!"

"REEEEEER!"

I figgered we might as well put Pete's theory to the test. I barked in his face. He hissed and yowled and humped up his back and pinned down his ears, and then, as if by magic, he began limping around, dragging a so-called wounded leg.

The front door flew open. Pete took time out from his acting career to give me a wink and a smile, and then he said, "I told you, Hankie."

Loper stepped out on the porch. "Holy cow, it's Hank. He made it with the cough syrup!" He came over and, you won't believe this, picked me up and gave me a big hug. "Good boy, Hank, good boy!"

I never would have dared believe that he would take me into the house. I mean, we know that I deserved such treatment, but miracles weren't common on our outfit. But that's exactly what he did.

Oh yes, and the best part came as he was carrying me towards the door. He tripped over the crippled cat, stumbled, yelled some harsh words, and booted old Pete right out into the snow.

Oh, how I loved it! Bravery and devotion to duty hath no greater rewards than to see the cat booted into a snowdrift.

Well, once we got into the house, I became the hero of the hour — of the day, in fact, or even the whole week. Or month.

Heck, the entire year.

Loper took me over to the woodstove and set me down in the place of honor. He stroked my head and scratched me behind the ears, and then he even scratched me on that spot just below my ribs, you

know, the spot that's hooked up to my back leg?

I've never understood exactly how and why that deal works, but when they scratch me there, my old back leg goes to kicking. Feels wonderful.

And whilst he was doing that, Sally May came into the room and wrapped me up in a towel. And get this: She dried me off with the towel!

Yes, her nose was wrinkled up and she said something about "cow lot" and "wet dog," as I recall her words, but by George, the old gal put some elbow grease into that towel-work and got me dried off.

Then they untied the medicine bag from around my neck and Sally May took the bottle back into Molly's room, and by that time Little Alfred had appeared on the scene.

He gave me a big hug and we wrestled around on the living room floor for a while. Then he blew in my face, as he seems to enjoy doing, and I licked him on the mouth.

Sally May walked in on that little exercise and put a stop to it. "Alfred, keep your face away from the dog's mouth! Do you want to get pellagra?"

He said, no, he didn't want to get pellagra, and neither did I, so we quit that game.

Oh, but there were plenty of other games to play. See, because of my heroic actions — and also because Little Alfred made a very effective begging presentation — I was allowed to remain inside the house for the rest of the storm.

Two whole entire days, if you can believe that!

Yes, Sally May insisted that I visit the Great Outdoors once every hour for "fresh air," as she put it, but that was okay with me.

Hey, me and Alfred played Horse, and Quail Hunt, and Ride the Bull, Hide Under the Bed, Dress-Up in Army Clothes, and my very favorite, Eat Crackers In The Closet.

And best of all, Little Molly got over her cough, and by the next morning, she was laughing and playing with the rest of us.

To preserve the happiness of the happy ending, I won't reveal what Sally May said when she caught us eating crackers in her closet, inside the tent we had made of her Sunday dress.

A guy doesn't have to tell everything he knows.

It was a wonderful blizzard and a happy ending.

Case closed.